First Blood

I0532957

FIRST BLOOD

RYAN J. PELTON

Rock House Publishing
Kansas City

First Blood

An Antique Assassin Crime Prequel

Book 4

This is a work of fiction. All of the characters, organizations, locations, and events portrayed in this novel are either product's of the author's imagination or are used fictitiously.

Second Edition

ISBN-13: 978-1-949420-08-1

Published, formatted, and designed by Rock House Publishing www.rockhousepublishing.com

For latest releases and updates visit ryanjpelton.com/fiction

Other Books by Author

Antique Assassin Crime series
Hired Gun (Book 1)
Stranger Danger (Book 2)
Color Blind (Book 3)
Stand Alone Novels
The Boardwalk
Shorts
Watched
Middle Grade Fiction (8-12)
The Ricky Rayburn Chronicles
Secrets of the Ambassadors
Mysterious Pirates of the Pacific (fall 2018)
Book 3 (winter 2018)

"Death is swallowed up in victory."
"O death, where is your victory?
O death, where is your sting?"
-1 Corinthians 15:55-56

1.

They say small towns can be stifling. LeClaire, Missouri pressed on my chest, leaving little room to breathe. When I registered for the Navy Seals, it was to explore the broader world. Certain decisions in life haunt you when you're old and reflective. Those riddled with regret. This wasn't one of those, despite it turning out different than I'd hoped.

I married my high school sweetheart, Lisa. It was a good decision and common in a town of less than twenty thousand people. The down home conservative types of LeClaire marry into the community before they are ready. It's the American thing to do. Lisa was a diamond in a sea of ugly stones, head cheerleader for East LeClaire High School. She had long blonde hair that would bounce off her tight behind as she danced around the gymnasium. Those same locks and buns drew me in, like a tractor beam, senior year. It was at a basketball game, against rival Greeley High, I recall.

Joining the Navy Seals was not a family decision. My father was in prison for robbery and murder. There were few military personnel in the O'Kane clan. Primarily because we emigrated from Ireland. Not my family, but my grandpa and great grandpa O'Kane. That's why I don't have an accent, but do have a certain proclivity toward beer. Oh, yeah, and a temper.

Recruiters of the military love to prey on small towns like LeClaire. Senior year I picked up a pamphlet, listened to a convincing Naval officer blabber about the opportunities the Navy offered. He appeared not a month older than me. Before I could blink, I was signing away my life to lands unknown.

Lisa was not on board. My one regret of applying for the Seals.

She wanted me to take classes at LeClaire Community College and become a mechanic or carpenter. I wanted to build an antique collecting business (which you'll hear more about later). Lisa claims I'm a cowboy always chasing the next shiny penny. The next adventure was an excuse to be irresponsible and avoid adult things like paying bills, changing diapers, and yearly doctor visits. Boring.

Military is a popular option for people in LeClaire because further education is not an option for many. Most hard working folks in our small town don't get through high school. My grandfather called his schooling The School of Hard Knocks. LeClaire-ites work as mechanics, carpenters, retail shop owners, or get lucky, and find a job at LeClaire Regional Hospital transferring patients, or doing administrative work. No doctors come from LeClaire. The government has to entice the big shot doctors to practice here, at the only hospital in town.

I chose the military... or did it choose me? I wasn't sure, but I needed to figure out life, and deal with the future, a future hazy like an early morning fog in Missouri.

Lisa dipped a French fry in ketchup and sipped on a vanilla milkshake at Rudy's Diner, the best greasy spoon in LeClaire. "Why the Navy Seals? Isn't that dangerous?"

I finished the last bite of bacon and avocado cheeseburger, wiped sauce from my lip, and sipped a Coke. "The Navy recruiter said my scores were higher than average. You need a minimum of seventy eight to enlist in the Navy. I got a ninety. He said I have promise."

She adjusted a clip holding her blonde hair back in a bun, "Those guys are in good shape. Can you handle the physical and mental side of the Seals? You were a star athlete in high school. But, that was small town sports, not division one like in Kansas City."

The lunch settled in my stomach and I let out a burp, "Sorry... too much Coke," I waved off Lisa, and remembered the football state championship junior year, "I'll be fine. This body is a machine," I said, displaying the chiseled six pack under my T-shirt.

Lisa slid the red basket of food remnants to the side, "Well, you will need to lay off the guacamole burgers and Coke. They ain't going to feed you Rudy's in basic training."

I slurped the Coke, "I've trained for months. This is fuel for the machine. I can out run and out think any of those dudes trying out for the Seals. I went to public school. Bank your sweet little life on it," I said, with a wink.

"I recall you sleeping through most of your senior year classes. Not the sharpest knife in the drawer. How's the knee?"

I reached down and rubbed the knee I had injured playing football senior year. "It's fine. Stiffens up when I run. My physical therapist said after surgery it would stiffen up once in a while. If I do my stretching and exercises, it'll hold up."

She nodded. "Your knee was in bad shape. Took a year of rehab to run again. You sure you don't want to enroll in community college? No chance of bullets buzzing your pretty face in Intro to Art History," Lisa said, leaning in for a kiss.

"We've talked about this, honey. I want to be a

Seal. The pinnacle of military service. Big dogs. If I am going to do this, I want to be the best."

"That's the problem. You want to be the best and leave me behind. We've been married less than a year. What am I going to do for all those months while you're gone?"

"Come on baby... don't give me a guilt trip. We dated for two years in high school. It's not like we barely know each other. Your mom and dad and brothers are here in LeClaire. You'll blink and I'll be home."

"Easy for you to say," Lisa said, rolling her eyes.

A wall of resistance built from across the table. I grabbed her hand, and caressed it, hoping to diffuse the reality of the US military taking me away from my new wife. "You'll be working at the power plant. You'll have family dinners with the folks. Before you blink, I'll be laying in bed next to you. And you know what that means?" I said, giving sexy eyes.

"Stop it. You're only getting the good loving because the military is stealing you away. I'm still mad at you. You're a cowboy chasing the next thing. I hope the military beats that out of you and parks you in my stable."

"Ooh, sexy stable talk. We can revisit that later."

Lisa held a hand over her mouth and blushed.

"That's why you love me. Who wants to live an ordinary life?"

Lisa peeled back her hand and gave a crooked

smile like she wanted to say something and couldn't get the words out.

"What's up?" I asked.

"I'm pregnant."

2.

The Greyhound bus blew dust and smoke into Lisa's face, as I turned her from the noise. She gripped my arms like it was the last time we'd ever touch. Her face was sullen and swollen from a night of crying and fighting.

Lisa lay against my chest and glanced up into my eyes. Her baby bump pressed against my stomach. I kissed her head, "Eight weeks is all. I have preparatory training, if all goes well, twenty-four more weeks. And then I'm done."

"What if you don't make it? SEALS are no joke. They're the best military unit in the world. You have a kid to think about. What is Plan B?" she leaned further into my chest.

"I have a Plan B. We can talk about it later."

"The junk collecting business?"

I smirked and tried to pretend she *wasn't* right. "Yes, among other ideas. Don't worry. The SEALS will work out. I'll get through my training. Make money. And our family will be back together. I promise."

A tall man with wide shoulders and a crew cut came up behind me. He saluted. I didn't know what to do and placed an awkward hand somewhere on my head. He gave a forced smile, "You O'Kane? Better get that salute in order or you won't last three days in basic."

"Yes, sir," I said, my stomach doing two somersaults, sweat bubbling up on the back of my T-shirt.

"Get in your goodbyes and the bus is leaving in five minutes. I don't tolerate tardiness."

I tried a second time with the salute and it came out more confident and a little less awkward. Lisa pushed me away and placed her hands akimbo on her hips. "Well, soldier. I'm guessing nothing can change your mind, now. You better get on that bus and come home in one piece. I got an O'Kane growing in my belly that needs his daddy," Lisa said, giving me a smile that was not formed and had an unsettling shape. The SEALS was breaking her heart and, yet, was something I had to do. The cowboy in me couldn't resist.

"O'Kane, it's been six minutes. One minute over five. If you want to get on my good side, get your ass on that bus," the officer said, pointing at the Greyhound, spit flying from both sides of his mouth.

I knelt down near the ground and kissed the baby bump and moved my way back up to Lisa. She grabbed my neck and squeezed with man-like pressure. I kissed her neck and turned her toward me and gave her a look over. She didn't say a word and disappeared into the truck

I glided down the aisle of the Greyhound and scoped out the competition. A short dark haired man greeted me near the middle of the bus. He was wearing a military issue uniform T-shirt which sagged on his small stature. "Names Freddy, Freddy Gillespie."

Freddy was an Italian from the southwest corner of Missouri. His family immigrated to the Midwest in the 50's and started a restaurant in Mason. Freddy had the hottest temper of any guy I'd ever met. Even for an Italian.

"Dexter O'Kane. I live here in LeClaire," I said, rubbing my knee through a pant leg.

"What's wrong with your knee?"

"Old football injury. Acts up when I work out."

"You been training hard? Heard the physical assessments are brutal."

I nodded. "How you feeling about the Seals? That officer freaked me out. He's intense."

Freddy waved me off, "He did the same thing to me. I wouldn't take it personally. It's the military's way of weeding out the pussies before they get to basic. You don't look like a pussy," he said, laughing and opening a black duffel bag, "You like beef jerky?"

I smiled and examined the slab of dehydrated meat, "You allowed to have that?"

"Don't give a shit. Can't leave home without it. Perfect snack. Low in fat and high in protein. What we need when they are running our asses into the ground. My dad makes it at home. Deer meat."

"Venison."

"What?"

"Never mind. I can do you one better," I said, reaching into my bag, "Almonds. Saltless, high in protein, and good fats. Perfect snack food. Devoured these nuts during training. That deer meat will cramp you up. Too much salt."

Freddy stared at me like I told him his mother died. "Seriously? That sounds bad."

I popped an almond in my mouth and opened a fist to share with Freddy, "Unsalted kind. Won't cramp you up. Saw a kid on my football team explode after eating deer meat."

Freddy chewed and gave a hard swallow. He paused for a beat, with wide eyes, and said, "Explode?"

I slapped him in the arm, "Just messing. But, leg cramps are the worst."

Freddy ate a couple more nuts, "That your old lady back there? She got one in the oven?"

I nodded and replayed the fight the night before, "High school sweetheart. Never imagined being a dad... Let alone married. I dreamed about a single guy life, not tied to any responsibility. Do anything

I want and whenever I want. Every guy's male fantasy, right?"

Freddy wagged his finger revealing a wedding band, "Hell, yeah. Damn women have us in the palms of their hands. Know we'll do whatever they want. How else does the human population keep going? Dumb ass guys like us always leading with their," he said, glancing down at his crotch.

I smiled knowing Lisa had me wrapped around her pregnant fingers.

Freddy leaned against the tall bus seat and gave out a sigh, "Mr. O'Kane. We have a long drive to Illinois. I am gonna rest my eyes and let these magical nuts do their work. Nice meeting you... and good night now."

I watched his eyes flutter to sleep with an accompanying snore. I did the same thing.

The baby and Lisa were giving me heartburn. Or maybe it was the almonds.

3.

The first seven weeks of training is what they call basic. It's anything but. We ran timed four mile runs to ensure we could cut the cake in real world combat. The SEALS are the best physically and mentally conditioned units in all the world for a reason. We jumped walls, swam laps, and did calisthenics until I almost puked.

Imagine basic training as high school football *hell week* on steroids. I made it through the first seven weeks with flying colors. Things intensified as weeks turned into months. The second seven weeks involved swimming. Not my strong suit. I could swim circles around my friends at LeClaire Lake during Missouri summers. These drunken wins didn't include officers climbing on my back, holding me under water, and lifting logs above my head as waves crashed into my torso. I'd take sipping Bud Lights on the shores of LeClaire Lake over SEALS training any day.

I treaded water in the middle of the pool and felt my legs getting fatigued. The instructor jumped into the Olympic sized pool and came up behind me like a shark on an unsuspecting child. "What you going to do now solider?" he asked, leaping onto my back and wrapping an arm around my neck, choking off my air, "Come on, O'Kane. Your comrades are in bad shape and sinking under the waves," the flat-topped instructor pressed further on my shoulders as I bobbed up and down, like a lure, gasping for air.

Water rushed into my mouth and penetrated my nostrils, forcing a burn in the back of my throat. I gave out a cough and tried to flip the captain over my back, hold up all the weight and find air.

To no avail.

Instructor Mays released his choke hold, pushed me aside, and we swam to the edge of the pool. The group of wannabe SEALS watched and grinned, knowing I didn't do well. Those bastards were hoping I'd fail so they could take my spot.

Mays paced the edge of the pool and stared down on the line of officers, "You pansies see what happened with O'Kane just now?" the instructor asked, moving from officer to officer and giving them a stare. He paced up and down the edge of the pool like a lifeguard looking for someone to save. That someone being me.

"In the heat of battle, things are unpredictable. A fellow SEAL might be drowning. Leg shot up.

Imagine waves of the Indian or Mediterranean Ocean pounding your head. You're in pursuit of a terrorist and running a night mission. When things get unpredictable, you need to focus. Be strong. Not like O'Kane. You want to die O'Kane?"

"No, sir," I said, with confidence.

The captain snapped a piece of gum and adjusted his shorts an inch above the knee. "That might not be what you want, O'Kane. But, that's what you got. Both dead. Enemy wins. You are part of the most skilled and dangerous military company in the world. Let this be a warning to all of you pansies. We train night and day because the world's safety is at stake. There are evil people around the world who want you dead. We can't have no pansies dying on my watch."

I held my head low and bobbed at the edge of the pool, wanting to go back to LeClaire after the tongue lashing. "But... you're lucky O'Kane. I'm in a generous mood today. I used you to be an example of what *not* to do. Let's learn from this and get better."

The entire company said, in unison, "Yes, sir."

Our instructing officer dismissed us to the locker room where we took showers and changed into dry uniforms. I came in last and didn't want to face the rest of the company. My pride was dangling like a tail between my legs.

I hid in a corner shower and avoided conversation.

A tall, blonde, broad shouldered solider came over to the bench where I was putting on my uniform. He leaned against the lockers and smiled like he was a high school punk looking for a fight, "What the hell was that O'Kane?"

I rolled my eyes and tried to avoid eye contact, buttoning the last buttons on my uniform, "What you want Waters?"

Denny Waters was the overconfident guy in the company who thought his shit didn't stink. A rich kid who grew up in suburbs of Chicago. Never failed a day in his life and didn't understand how blue collar people lived. Like the hardworking people of LeClaire. Captain of the football team, student council President, and best GPA at his school. His dad was a successful lawyer and his mother a doctor. I assumed they wiped their asses with hundred dollar bills.

"O'Kane, you're making us look bad. I don't want you fucking things up with those shenanigans back there," Waters said, propping a muscular leg on the bench.

"Mind your business. I'm doing my best. Swimming is not my strong suit," I said, standing eye level with Waters, and jamming my shirt into the front of my pants and cinching the belt, "Why does this concern you? If I fail, it's one more spot for these guys, who cares?"

"We win and fail as a unit. Your little episode

back at the pool doesn't bode well for those taking this seriously. Guys who want to be SEALS."

I inched closer to Waters and smiled, "You don't think I'm serious? A game? I recall carrying your ass in the log run. Held that massive piece of wood above your head when you cramped up. Too much salt in the diet?"

A crowd of dudes formed, some half naked and some in full uniform. Waters gave an awkward smile and his face turned a shade of red, knowing a crowd was forming and what I had said was true, "Maybe. SEALS are swimmers. If you can't swim, you need to head back to Hicksville," he said, licking his lips, and looking for affirmation from the dozen guys moving in around the altercation.

"Listen, rich boy. You've never worked an honest day in your life. Born with a golden spoon in your ass. I might not be the strongest swimmer in the unit. But, I work my ass off every single day, and all these guys can vouch for that. Next time a log gets too heavy for you, don't cry for my help," I turned around and pointed at the men in a circle, "We are in this together. I don't need no dick measuring contest."

Waters held up his hands in surrender, backed up a step and gave a forced grin, "You got me all figured out, country boy. Figure my folks are wealthy and everything comes easy. Well, you don't know shit about me, my family, or what hard work is all about. I'll run circles around you. And, swim cir-

Ryan J. Pelton

cles around you, which we all know is easy after the pathetic display in the pool," he said, nodding to the group.

I leapt at Waters and caught him with a forearm just under his chin. He slammed against the lockers and bounced back toward me with a fist cocked. As I lowered in a football stance to attack for a second time, my foot slipped on the wet cement.

I felt my knee twist to the right and a shooting pain shot through my right leg. The pain left me crumpled, to the right of Waters, on the floor. He bounced up and down like a prize fighter, "Get up pussy? Let me punch in your face and see who the tough guy around here is?"

I grabbed the knee and winced and tried to play off an explosion of pain, "Go to hell. A waste of time."

"What's wrong with your leg?" he said, leaning over me and examining me caressing the inside portion of my knee.

"Slipped on the water and tweaked it. I'm fine."

"That's too bad. You need all the help you can get with the swimming. Ducks need their flippers," he said, looking at the other guys and smiling.

The crowd of guys dispersed and an animated man emerged into the center of the chaos. "What the fuck is going on soldiers?"

Waters put his hands at his side, "Nothing, sir. O'Kane slipped, and I was helping him up."

I looked at Waters and rolled my eyes and looked

back to the officer, "Yes, sir. Slipped on the wet cement. No big deal."

"Why are you grabbing your knee, son? You need to see a doctor? That won't be good if you want to make it through the next stage. You need help with the swimming. Bad leg hurts your chances of becoming a SEAL."

I nodded. "It'll be fine. Old injury, just a sprain."

The officer pulled me up from the ground and glanced over at Waters, "Whatever this shit is needs to stop. Better not find out you guys are lying to a commanding officer. That won't be good for anyone," he said, snapping his gum, "I got my eye on both of you. Don't cross me."

We both saluted.

He disappeared through the back of the locker room and I realized the pain in my knee was worse than expected. That wasn't helping my cause.

4.

The bartender poured a Jack and Coke and examined my outstretched leg on the barstool. "Leg's supposed to go under the stool. Ice helping?" the slender man asked, wiping down a beer glass with a stained towel.

I smiled and readjusted the bag of ice hugging my swollen knee. "Thanks for the tip. Between the ice and Jack things will get brighter in a few minutes," I said, saluting the drink slinger.

The jukebox cranked *Communication Breakdown* by Led Zeppelin and a sea of middle-aged couples swayed on the beaten wooden dance floor. *Zippy's* was one of the few bars in the small town in Illinois. The Naval Preparatory School located at the Great Lakes Base.

I'd escaped to put down a few and hoped the fire in my knee would subside before training the next morning. My self-confidence was waning with every dip in the pool.

The bartender stacked glasses in a plastic bin behind the slick counter, "SEALS training?"

I nodded. "How'd you know?"

"T-shirt gave it away."

I glanced down at the military issue SEALS tee, with matching navy blue sweatpants. "Supposed to be a covert mission. Bad sign of things to come?" I said, sipping on the Jack, as it warmed my body.

"What happened to the knee?" bartender asked, refilling a bowl with mixed nuts.

I gripped the bag of ice and slipped it off my knee, "Old football injury. Swells up time to time. I'd take two-a-days in August over SEALS training any day."

"Jack and Coke. Ice pack. Looks more serious than an old pig skin injury. You have it checked out?"

"You a doctor?"

"No," he said, smiling and drying his hands on an apron, "Tried out for SEALS. I've seen that face."

"What face?"

"Those tired eyes. A look of defeat, anger, confusion. Five years ago, I had a face like yours."

"I ain't defeated. Knee's fine. A little ice, Jack. Back at it tomorrow, like nothing happened. What's your story?"

"How many Jack's you planning to put down?" he asked, glancing at his watch, "Married my high school sweetheart. Wanted to make a difference in the world. Applied to join SEALS. Failed before I started," he said, pointing at his eyes, and sliding thin framed glasses to the edge of his nose.

"What's wrong with your eyes?"

"Don't have 20/20. Perfect vision or bye to the SEALS. Must not have read the fine print."

I sipped on the Jack and swirled the little red straw around in the brown liquid, "We're a lot alike. High school sweethearts that is. How long you been married?"

"Divorced, made it two years. Split up after I failed the SEALS exam. You?"

"Nine months. Wife ain't happy I'm here. Kid on the way. Thinks I'm running from something. A cowboy looking for the next ride. "

"Have to be a little wild to consider the SEALS. Cowboy spirit is a must. I understand the predicament, man. When I failed the SEALS, I was so distraught I never left Illinois. Didn't have the guts to face my hometown. Another kid from any town USA with a bleak future. Small towns can be brutal."

I nodded. "Preaching to the choir, brother. LeClaire, Missouri, you?"

"Kearney, Nebraska. Population six thousand."

"Real small... Twenty thousand in LeClaire, if you count surrounding counties. A stuffy and isolating place. I'm a cowboy looking for time away from the ranch. Who knows? If this knee doesn't get better, I might find a new place in Illinois. Need a roommate?" I asked, with a wink.

The bartender chuckled.

I tossed the ice bag on the counter and sipped the last drop of Jack. "Love to commiserate a little longer but I need to call the wife before she files for divorce. Pay phone in the back?"

Bartender pointed to a back hallway with a bank of bathrooms and pay phones.

I limped to the back of the bar, climbed on a stool and winced, the knee throbbing. I tossed a couple quarters in the slot, "Hey, babe. Just checking in. How are things?"

Lisa answered and sounded extra bubbly, "Got a promotion at work. Power plant said I was the best secretary they've ever had. Gave me an extra dollar an hour."

I slapped the side of the payphone, "That's great, baby. I'm sure you're working your ass off. Told you you wouldn't miss me. Too busy with work."

"You are forgettable. I met a guy who's taking *real* good care of me. A gentle lover," she said, snorting in the phone, trying to hold back a laugh.

"I see your sense of humor hasn't changed. Glad you have a man-toy to keep you warm."

"You will have to step up your game when you get home. When you coming back?"

"Middle of training. If I make it through this portion, it should only be a few more months."

"Months? That's a long time. You will miss the birth."

"Never in a million years. I'll be in that hospital room ready to catch him or her."

"Dexter, it's a child. Not a football. Something I need to tell you," Lisa said, with a tinge of hesitation in her voice.

"How are things with the baby? Everything all right?"

"Had a five month doctor checkup. Doctor Rogers has concerns."

I slid off the stool and leaned against the payphone to hear Lisa, amidst Jimmy Hendrix *Purple Haze*, "What kind of concerns?"

"The heart beat is weak. They don't think it's fatal but want it to get stronger," Lisa said, choking up, "I miss you Dex. I'm scared."

My body warmed and trembled with nerves, "Are these doctors any good? What can we do?"

"Nothing. We wait. They'll keep an eye on him and listen to the heart every week. Hope for improvement."

"Did you say *him*? We having a boy?"

"Maybe... Maybe not. I didn't find out. We agreed, remember?"

"You hiding something? Does he have balls?"

"Is that all you care about? I told you our child might die. Have a little sympathy."

"I'm sorry. But, every man hopes for a boy. They

think about the things their dad's did with them. Fishing, hunting, nudie bars."

"Grow up... besides you didn't have a dad."

"All the things you *wished* they'd done with you."

"You think about that kind of stuff, Dex? That's sweet."

"Not just a pretty face, honey."

"Not sure if junior has man-parts. But, after the last comment, I'll dump my boyfriend. It'll be hard," Lisa said, trying to hold back a laugh.

"Very funny. I'm enjoying a little sweetie here in Illinois. I'll break the news to her..." I said, scanning the bar of older women.

"You don't got no time for a woman. Got to focus on passing SEAL training and getting your ass back home. My bed gets too cold I will look for a man to warm it up. How's training going?"

I hesitated and glanced at the knee, "Not bad. I'm running well and conditioning is good," I paused on the line, "Swimming has been tough."

"Not surprising. You ain't no dolphin in the water."

"Hey, easy. Thanks for confidence. I can swim. Not great, but good enough. Swim circles around you."

"Everything is not a competition. You're right. That wasn't fair. But, you are not exactly a duck in the water. More like a dog."

"My instructor's been working with me. You'd

be surprised at the progress. More duck-like every day. I have another problem."

"What's that? They don't have life jackets?"

"No. Ease up on the jokes. My knee is bothering me."

"The football knee?"

"Yeah. I tweaked it in the pool. Slowing me down and swelling up like crazy."

"You getting treatment? Officers know?"

"Icing it, now. And, no. I can't tell them.

"You got to be honest. They'll understand."

"No way. If they see weakness, it's over. The other guys don't know either. They'll tell the commanding officers and I would be done. Only a few spots open for the SEALS."

"You're a prideful man Dexter William O'Kane. Never can admit when you need help. The cowboy who needs nobody and nothing. Suck up the pride and tell someone. That's all I will say."

I didn't respond. "We'll see. Good to hear from you, baby. Tell me how junior is doing next appointment. And I'll call you again soon."

"Love you, Dex."

"Ditto."

We hung up the phone, and I realized the Jack and Coke had kicked in. The conversation about complications with the baby hit me in the gut. A tear welled up in my eye and I gripped the stool and leaned against the phone.

My knee throbbed and my heart hurt. I missed

Lisa but something inside wasn't eager to get back home.

The cowboy spirit's strong.

5.

"**O**" Kane, get your ass moving if you wanna be a SEAL," the officer barked in my ear, as I jumped out of the pool, and leapt over a wall. My knee was miraculously holding together from ice, Advil, and Jack.

The final stages of training were in my sights.

I turned the corner of the pool and left the indoor facility to head to an outdoor course. Freddy Gillespie waited near a log about ten feet long. He hoisted it with help of a couple other cadets and gave a sheepish grin, "We're gonna do it. Carry this damn tree to the finish line and we're in. Let's do this," he said, giving me a wink.

A group of cadets came up behind the log and gave us enough power to secure it, with trembling hands, above our heads. We entered the frigid lake water. We grunted with all our might, trying to ignore the weight and lack of air in our lungs. With every step, my arms weakened, and the knee loosened. The tendons shifted side to side like a bowl of spaghetti.

I glanced at the knee every few feet and the sweat of the grunting cadets splashed my face.

A cadet yelled out, "Go boys. We're almost to the end. Navy pride, let's do it. Hoorah."

"Hoorah," I said, with reluctance, and couldn't stop watching the knee.

A second officer cried out in pain as his arms wavered under the weight of the log. I called out, "Men, we're here for a reason. Protect and serve this great country. The end is near. Hoorah," the men repeated in unison.

The waves crashed up against our chests and the log swayed side to side, almost falling into the lake. Arms strained and veins popped as the last stretches of the course were in sight.

Spit and groaning and yelling filled the Illinois air and the coldness of the water was masked by adrenaline.

And, then it happened. The pain of all pains shot through the tendons, cartilage, and bones of my knee, the injury I'd hoped wouldn't revisit. A fire shot though my knee, and it exploded with pain. I dropped out from hoisting the log and fell to the side. It happened so fast none of the soldiers noticed I'd fallen into the waters below and was crying out in pain.

I glanced up from the shallow waters and could see the men marching with the log bobbing along.

Freddy Gillespie attempted to peek back at me flailing in the lake.

I grabbed the surgically repaired knee on the leg that carried my high school football team to a championship junior year. An appendage needing ACL and MCL surgery senior year a few short years before. I floated on my back and stared into the clear sky and the pain dissipated for a moment. Things went silent and I could hear the faint echoes of *Hoorah* and cheering. The refrain I'd never say again.

The silence and moment of peace replaced with the numbing waters of the shallow lake water. I crawled to the shore with the injured leg dangling like it was wounded in battle. I turned on my side and lay in the sand, not sure what to do next.

A bird flew over and it reminded me of LeClaire and summers near Lake LeClaire where I had learned to swim. I desired home and simultaneously feared what might await me. A wife and child. A small town with limited options of a future. Being a SEAL crowded out a desire for a family. I knew it was wrong. But, now, family was all I had.

The voice of a man yelling in my direction snapped me back into reality. I ignored the sound and stared at the sun and birds. Maybe if I ignored it, I'd awake and find it all a dream. No such luck.

"O'Kane. What in the hell are you doing? Getting a tan?" the officer barked giving my injured body a look over.

I pointed to the knee.

He knelt down as the waters splashed against us. "What am I looking at?"

"Knee," I said, wincing in pain.

"What about it?"

"It's done. Tore it up."

The officer shook his head and leaned down and grabbed me around the midsection. He lifted my tired body to a standing position. I kept the bad knee bent and tried to steady myself. He called on a walkie-talkie for an officer to come and assist.

"Sorry, son. Hate to see this happen to a good soldier. Your shooting is some of the best we've seen. The swimming not that good, but you were making progress. I don't know if you'll come back from this."

I hobbled across the shore of the lake like it was a year long journey to nowhere.

A group of officers greeted me at the entrance of the training center. The SEALS in training were off to the side slapping each other's backs and two of them glanced in my direction. Freddy pretended not to see me and looked in the other direction, getting back to the celebration.

On a beach in Illinois, my dreams of becoming a Navy SEAL swept away with the tide.

I headed to LeClaire without the honor of protecting our great country. Instead, I needed to figure out how to provide for a wife and kid with no education and no prospects.

Not the homecoming I was hoping for. Maybe I needed to call Uncle Hank.

6.

The Greyhound bus slowed to a stop and dust spit from underneath the tires. I gathered my duffel bag and peeked out the bus window to see Lisa waving.

I gave a nod and realized I wasn't ready to enter civilian life. The SEALS were a bust and the thought of married life and a new child created low level nausea. More burden and less joy.

Lisa glided toward the bus as I leapt to the ground and gave a forced smile. "My man. Meet your baby boy," she said, handing me a small human wrapped in blankets. It looked like a burrito only cuter.

I dropped my bag on the dusty ground, tears flooding from my face in an unexpected and uncontrollable way. "I'm sorry. I failed you and the family."

Lisa leaned into my babbling mess and tried to protect the baby boy from getting smashed. "Dexter, what are you talking about? You did the best you could. Who would ever think a knee would shatter your dreams? You're home and that's what matters."

I pushed back from Lisa, wiped snot from my face, and kissed the forehead of Spencer. "Dad is sorry. I wanted you to have a SEAL for a father. I guess you'll have a loser like the rest of the people in LeClaire."

Lisa smacked my shoulder, "Shut up. You're not a loser. The people of LeClaire aren't losers. These are our people, my people. How dare you talk like that?"

I gave a raised eyebrow to Lisa and didn't want to defend what I felt was right and true, "We all have our opinions. Don't know what the hell I'm supposed to do now. No education, no job, and mouths to feed."

Lisa forced Spencer into my arms and I wobbled, holding the child in my arms, "Hope we're more than mouths to feed. Good to see you're happy to be home. I haven't seen you in months, and not to mention, we just had a premature baby. Sorry to be a dream killer," Lisa said, shaking her head, and staring off into the distance.

I kicked at the dirt with my boot and found Spencer comforting. He opened his swollen blue eyes and gave a blank stare. I peeked at Lisa, "I'm emotional right now. Don't know what I'm supposed to do, next. Give me time."

"What you do next is love your wife and kid. Enjoy the time with us. You'll figure it out."

"Everything all right with Spencer? The heart stuff and all?"

"Yep. He came a month early. A healthy baby boy. Thanks for asking," Lisa said, snarling her lip.

"Come on, baby. No sympathy for a wounded soldier. I worked my ass off and was yards from the next stage of the SEALS. It's hard right now. Loosen up," I said, with a snarl.

"You have a day to throw a pity party. Tomorrow we get back the old Dexter. Then we find you a job."

I handed Spencer back to Lisa and picked up the duffel. "Pity party today only, right? Not tomorrow?" Lisa eyed me, shocked I'd take up the offer so abruptly. "I'm going to O'Malley's for a drink."

I held up a thumb and waved down a Honda Civic leaving the bus depot. They looked harmless.

Lisa froze in the middle of the depot with Spencer in hand. She watched, with mouth wide open, as the car passed her face.

The bus spit out a plume of dirt and vanished toward the highway.

***

I sipped a Jack and Coke and surprised myself with how numb I must have become to leave my wife and baby in the lurch. A chubby guy, with two lonely hairs at the back of his scalp, waddled to the counter and smiled. "How goes it, Dexter? Aren't you a little young to be in here?"

I waved at a younger bartender, with more hair, washing a glass in the corner. "Charlie did me a solid. Owed me one for messing with me freshman year."

Charlie Babcock was the older brother of a good friend in high school. He was four years older than me and legal drinking age. I was not and still a year out from becoming a real adult. Small towns aren't as strict on the drinking laws.

"Charlie said it was okay, huh? I'll let it slide this time. Heard the military sent you home with a bum knee."

I nodded and glanced down at the knee in a brace that needed surgery when the swelling went down. I'd been through the routine before and wasn't looking forward to the six months of rehab and daily pain. My motivation was no longer getting healthy to finish senior year with back-to-back championships. I needed a functional knee to enter the adult world of paying bills and taking care of a wife and baby. It sounded less and less like a dream and more like a nightmare.

"Rumor is true. No medal of honor and hometown hero, I guess," I said, twirling the brown liquid with a straw.

"Well, kid, LeClaire is proud of you none the less. Few ever leave this town unless they are in the military. At least you can tell your kids you tried."

I nodded thinking about the tiny human cuddled in Lisa's arms back at the homestead. Not having a dad added pressure to wanting to make my kid proud. Who wants a dad working the power plant for ten bucks an hour the rest of his life? Working at Uncle Hank's auto shop?

A bushy haired man nestled into the stool next to me and plopped a rusty box on the counter. I took a second look and wondered what his deal was. "Nice box," I said, with a sheepish grin.

The man nodded and ordered a beer and stared at the counter not appearing social. "Where'd you get it?"

Bartender slapped a napkin and a beer on the counter and the mystery man shook his head like he'd had a long day or long life. "Get what?"

"The box."

"On a pick."

"Pick? Like boogers?"

"No. I'm a picker. I find rusty gold and sell it to interested customers."

The picker piqued my interest, and I tried to probe for more information. "You make a living picking boogers, I mean, rusty gold?"

"Yep," he said, sipping the beer and not making eye contact, "Done pretty well."

I left the stool and limped over to the man and examined the rusty box. "What's so special about this old thing? I've seen a million of these."

"Good for you."

"I did some picking when I was a kid. Don't think we called it such. My friends and I used to ride our bikes out behind the landfill and find rusty treasures. We'd sell the junk at garage sales and to neighbors. I guess it was my first business. Found lots of boxes like this one," I said, turning it over.

He gave me a deadly stare like I'd tripped an old lady, "One man's junk... another man's treasure, I like to say. Please don't touch. It's paying my mortgage this month," he said, warming up to the conversation.

"Mortgage? You paying ten dollars a month? No way in hell this box is worth anything. If this box is paying your mortgage, get me in on the action," I said, limping back to the stool.

"Thousand."

"Thousand, what?"

"The box and the mortgage."

I turned to see if anyone in O'Malley's was watching this interaction because this guy was crazy. "Get out of town. You be ripping people off."

"Maybe more," the man said, sipping a beer, and popping a peanut in his mouth.

I slapped a twenty dollar bill on the counter. "You prove the box is worth a grand, I will give you my last twenty dollars."

The man pushed the money aside. "Don't want your money, kid. Come by the house tomorrow and I'll prove it. 1064 Riverside Drive. House on the left."

I scribbled the number on a napkin and could feel my insides coming to life. The thought of making a grand on a rusted out box intrigued my skeptical soul. I gave a smirk and sipped the last of the Jack and Coke. "Prove it tomorrow. Tonight I will enjoy the pity party. See you then."

The bushy haired man raised an eyebrow and did not understand what I said. He disappeared into the parking lot.

I have no prospects and few employable job skills. Maybe beginning of something good. Plan B.

7.

I picked up a bowl of Frosted Flakes and ignored Lisa dancing around the small kitchen in our rented apartment. Not an apartment. More of a tiny house designed for abnormally sized people next to a real sized house in the back of Uncle Hank's lot. Homecoming from the military got more depressing with each passing day.

She grabbed a spatula and lip synced to "*Hit Me with Your Best Shot.*"

I sipped my coffee and said, "Why you so chipper?" trying to not lead on that I enjoying the singing and dancing of Lisa.

She paused, placed her hands on her hips, and grinned ear to ear. Her perfect teeth and a pink tank top and cutoff jean shorts were highlighting a body not affected by a tiny human coming out of it months earlier, "My man's home. We have a new baby. What's not to be happy about?"

"Yeah. Life's grand."

Lisa glided over to the round kitchen table, a hand-me-down from her folks, and widened her arms across the dented surface, "Get over it. Move on. The SEALS are done. Sorry the dream of fighting bad guys vanished with the knee," Lisa glanced at the Ace wrap around my gimpy leg, "I need you here, and you need a job. Did you talk to Uncle Hank?"

I nodded. "Being a wrench monkey is not my thing. My step-dad never showed me how to work on cars."

"How do you know it's not your thing? You going to apply for auto shop classes, at LeClaire Community College, today?"

I twirled the soggy flakes and sipped cold coffee, "No. I'm exploring other options. A Plan B."

Lisa smacked my head with the spatula. She curled a lip like a pit bull ready to pounce, "Better not be talking about the junk business. No husband of mine is collecting people's trash for a living. You need to talk to my uncle. He makes good money fixing cars. Selling junk ain't going to put shoes on your babies. Hank owns two houses; he must be doing okay, right?"

I scanned the house not bigger than four hundred square feet, "Half a house."

"What?"

"Nothing."

"Not selling junk. Rusty gold."

"Rusty what?"

"Pickers don't call it junk. Rusty gold. The older the better."

"Pickers? Like boogers?"

I held in a laugh, "No, pickers, like antique collectors. Doesn't matter. I met a guy."

"A guy... You gay?" Lisa said, pretending to lick the spatula.

"Not that kind of guy. At O'Malley's yesterday. He gave me some ideas for making money."

Lisa glared at me, "Oh, yeah. When I let you have your pity party? Hope you enjoyed it. Tell me about your boyfriend."

I laughed and thought she was funny, "An old guy told me how he sells rusty gold and makes a lot of money."

"Rusty gold?"

"Antiques. The stuff I used to collect when I was a kid."

"Those old bicycles and cans? How you going to make money collecting that junk, rusty gold, whatever...?"

I became animated and ignored the variety of confusing facial expressions Lisa was making like doing math or pinching a loaf, "He showed me this old rusty box at the bar. Just got it on a pick. I thought it was a piece of junk not worth the metal used to make it. He told me it would pay his mortgage. How about that?"

"Was the mortgage five bucks?"

"That's what I said. A grand."

Lisa hit me, "You stupid, Dex? Ain't no rusty box worth a thousand bucks. Go out the back door and find a ton of rusty shit on my uncle's lot. Worthless. Sounds like a scam. Like when those Bible salesmen come round and use God's name to make money. Prey on the old women."

I waved her off. "He ain't no Bible salesman. Been making money, for years, selling rusty gold. He invited me to his house. Show me the ropes."

"You sure he ain't gay? Old man inviting you over to check out his rusty box," Lisa said, caressing the back of my bed head, and kissing my neck, "You got everything you need at home."

"Easy, tiger. Keep talking like that, I will leave the old guy for you."

Lisa shook her butt and pointed at her firm buns. "You'd never leave all of this."

"Enough already. I'm going over to his house this afternoon. He will show me his collection. Tell me about the business and how I can start my own."

"Wait... Excuse me. No way in hell you are starting a business. You need something stable. Like a mechanic."

"An antique collecting business can be stable. Find some rusty boxes, build it up. This is my Plan B. I think this could be exactly what we're looking for."

"What *you're* looking for. Talk to my uncle and

see about a mechanic apprenticeship. Sounds more stable. Everybody needs their car fixed. Not everyone wants to buy junk."

Lisa had a point. I was no business man and was not sure how anyone could make money selling rusty gold. But the cowboy in me wanted to see what it was all about. I wanted the freedom to make my own hours and not be tied down to working the power plant or doing oil changes. The old guy paying his mortgage with a rusty box intrigued me. I needed to follow the trail and see if he was blowing smoke up my broke ass.

"Make you a deal. If the gay rusty-gold-selling-guy is not up to snuff, I will talk to Uncle Hank. Consider classes at the community college."

Lisa gave a half hearted nod that made it clear she wasn't pleased with Plan B. She glided back into the kitchen and cranked up the music. She pointed the spatula in my direction and continued lip syncing, "Cry in your Frosted Flakes if you have to. I'm going to have a good day. Tell me how the gay junk collector is. I'll call Uncle Hank and give him a heads up to expect you," she said, giving a smile that could make me do anything.

I gave a second glance at her firm behind. Anything except become a mechanic.

8.

I banged my head on the steering wheel of a rust bucket. It was not a car in the ways I'd define it. I borrowed it from Uncle Hank and he had given a hard time for not wanting to be a mechanic. By the looks of the beaten down 1983 Datsun, I wasn't sure any mechanic could salvage the thing. It huffed and coughed like my Grandmother Ruth's emphysema before she died. The road showed beneath my feet, like driving a Flintstone car.

Driving the beater motivated my hope the rusty gold collector was legitimate and there was a possible future of picking down the road. I wasn't providing for the family. Men supposed to be protectors and providers. We lived in a tiny house, practically free on Hank's dime, the car was a loner, and, if it made it home, it would be a miracle equal to Jesus' resurrection. I wasn't protecting or providing for anybody.

I arrived at a white ranch style home, decorated with a sea of gnomes and miniature windmills around the perimeter of the house. I wiggled the handle of the door and gave it a shove as it had frozen shut. The driver door yawned opened and howled like a wolf in the night. I turned and scoped out the massive five acres of rusted out barns, car ports, and sheds, most likely filled with rusty gold.

I gave a smile at the possibility *of* scoring rusty gold for a living.

The bushy-haired old man greeted me on the porch and ignored my outstretched hand. "You're late."

I waved my John Deere hat and gave a confused smile at the absence of the normal cultural greeting of a handshake. "Sorry, the car can't go above fifty on the highway."

He ignored my explanation.

"Beautiful day, ain't it?" I said, trying to drum up small talk.

"Depends how you see it."

"How long you lived here?"

"Longer than your life."

I rolled through a variety of questions in my head to dislodge the awkwardness and abruptness of the old man not wanting to answer my questions.

I took off my hat and pointed it at a red barn in the distance, "I bet that barn is full of mortgage payments."

"Huh?"

"Remember, at the bar. You said..."

He looked me over like I was wearing a dress and had a monkey on my shoulder. "Picking ain't for the faint of heart. You got to have thick skin and big balls."

I glanced at my crotch and arm, "Okay..."

"People gonna try to rip you off. Don't let em. Study market and what sells."

The old man walked away and said nothing to get my attention. I followed like a kid trying to get a famous athletes autograph. "Study the markets... Careful people don't rip you off. Anything else?"

The old man unsheathed a pistol from his hip and pointed it between my eyes, "Protect yourself. Crazy people be living on the back roads of America."

I raised my hands and was sure I had soiled my jeans. My heart beat into my neck but I tried to play it cool, "Great advice. You meet any crazies when picking? Bet you got stories," I said, trying to keep the conversation going.

"Last week a guy pulled a knife. Said I was ripping him off. I blew a hole in his face."

"Oh, shit. You did?"

"No. Thought about it for a minute. Another rule, don't kill, unless necessary."

"You kill anybody on the back roads?" I asked fearful of the answer, knowing nobody could hear my screams in this remote part of LeClaire.

Silence.

My knees trembled and the only thought in my mind was *crazy* was standing in front of me. I took a deep breath and realized, if I had a hole in my chest, I'd bleed out with the closest hospital twenty miles away. "Besides the crazies and watching for people ripping you off, can a guy like me support a family picking?"

He re-holstered the gun, and tenderness washed over his face like confusion by an unexpected emotion. "I did, for a time."

I lowered my hands and brushed my crotch with the back of my hands to make sure I hadn't wet myself, "You have family?"

"Did."

I probed further, "They live here?"

"Died a couple years back."

I paused at the unexpected response and wasn't sure what to say to the grizzled man, "Sorry. That must be tough."

He tried to resist a tear that was forming under his gold rimmed police style sunglasses, "You want to know how?"

"You don't have to tell me."

"Used picking money to buy a boat. We were out on LeClaire Lake. Some drunken asshole slammed into us."

A tear slithered down his cheek, and he didn't change his tone, "I'm the only one that lived. You can make a living. But, it'll cost you."

I wanted to hug him for a second but realized it would not be a good idea after he aimed a gun between my eyes. I put my hands in my pocket. "Well, for what it's worth, I bet they were great people and you have a nice place here."

He ignored the comment and kept walking further into the yard. I paused for a beat, confused whether to follow, leave, or change my underwear.

I followed.

He kept talking with his back to me and I tried to keep up with a quick pace for an old guy. "I'll show you where the real money is at."

We arrived at a red barn and he fiddled with the padlock and yanked open the wide double doors. A plume of dust shot in our faces and we both coughed.

The dust cleared, and I peeked into the barn. There were half a dozen rows of motorcycles, cars, trailers, bicycles, trucks, and tractors, perched in symmetrical rows in the barn. "My mortgage payments."

I walked the line of rusty vehicles and stopped in my tracks to examine a 1923 Indian motorcycle. "That'll make you fifteen grand in an afternoon," the old man said with a half grin.

I moved to the next vehicle, a John Deere tractor parked to the side of one line of cars. "That'll make you twenty. 1956 was a good year for tractors."

I shook my head and tried to compute the numbers he shot back at me. I hadn't seen that kind of money in my short life. "If you're telling the truth, and I think you are, where do you find rusty gold?"

He pulled up a metal chair sitting to the side of the cars and waved me over to sit in an adjacent one. His face became sullen as he took off the sunglasses. "That's why we do this."

"Do what?"

"Pick. It's all about the hunt."

"So, where do you find these money makers?"

"They find you."

The old man leapt from his chair like bitten by a snake and left me alone in the barn. I tried to follow, but he disappeared back into the house.

I hopped in the rust bucket, smiled toward the house and glanced at the barn. The words of the man, *it's all about the hunt,* summed up everything in my head. No idea where to hunt. Or, what the hunt was. But think I had found a new job.

I needed money and Lisa needed to understand mechanic school was not in the cards.

9.

The sign on the abandoned butcher shop hung low and swayed in the Missouri wind. I walked up and down the sidewalk and examined my future.

A heavyset man wearing a Missouri State sweatshirt crossed his arms and sipped on a Diet Cherry Coke. He cocked his head, "How in the hell you pay for this dump?"

"Your mom. I promised her some favors... if you know what I mean?" I said, licking my lips.

John smacked me in the head and sipped on his forty-four ounce drink, "Shut the hell up. Not in a good place right now. Momma jokes aren't helping."

"Kicked out of college. Is that hard to do?"

"Not really. Just don't show up to class and run a gambling ring out of your dorm room. You'd be surprised how badly they want you gone."

John Wood had been my best friend from life's

first cry. He had lived down the street from my family, attended the same schools, and separated for the first time when I had left for the SEALS. He had headed off to Missouri State to study biology. Everything was true about getting kicked out of school. He had made big bucks, on the side, running Friday night poker games. Biology and chemistry didn't hold his attention. He was the smartest guy in our high school and got bored easily. He had figured being a doctor would be a good challenge. Modern education was too constraining for John though. He needed room to experiment and think and not confined by authoritarian leadership. At least, that's what he tells me.

John wiped an inch of dirt from the front window of the old shop. "How did you pay for this place? Jimmy Hoffa living under those busted floor boards?"

"Cashed out my life's savings. Money from when mom died. I had an account I couldn't touch until something important came along, first house, school, or buying my dead grandpa's butcher shop. Lisa doesn't know, keep it under your hat," I said, feeling a butterfly in the stomach over knowing *a* conversation needed to happen sooner than later.

"About the money or shop?"

"Both. That's a conversation I have been avoiding like the plague. She wants me to take auto shop classes at the community college. This is my Plan B."

"Auto shop, that's rich. You can't change a light bulb. I don't pretend to understand the ladies. But, this might be the dumbest thing you've ever done. Lisa will beat the shit out of you. How's it being a daddy? You're going to mess that kid up."

"Why can't I be a good dad?"

"You didn't have one."

"So... you had five dads. Not comparable."

"What does that mean?"

"You're not exactly mayor of this town."

"Give me time. I'm only twenty. Your dad bailed when you were six. Why won't you do the same?"

"That's a path I hope not to follow. I hated not having a real dad. I learned shit from my step dad."

"How to be a dick and cheat on your wife?"

"No. Other stuff. Like how to cook steak. Shoot squirrels. What else do you need to become a mature adult?"

John ignored the comment and scanned the inside of the old butcher shop. "Hope you didn't pay too much for this roach playground. Got lots of work to do."

"I negotiated a good price with the owner. I told him my granddad had owned the place and his last wish before he died was to keep shop in the family. Played the sympathy card."

"Did your granddad really own this dump?"

"Yep. Emigrated from Ireland and opened a butcher shop. He served the people of LeClaire beef, pork, and cold cuts for fifty years. Died after I was born."

"Why didn't your family take it over?" John asked.

"The meat business is tough. Wal-Mart and other grocery stores put the little guys out. Can't compete on cheap meats, I guess."

John nodded. "What's your plan for the meat shop? Are you going to be a butcher?"

"Picker."

"Like boogers?"

"No, dummy. Antique collector. We search the byways and highways of Missouri for rusty gold. Like we did as kids. One man's junk another man's treasure. I've always wanted to do picking for a living."

John sipped the last drops of Coke and paused for a beat, "You mean the old bicycles we used to steal and fix up? That was your dream job? Since when..."

"Since I met an old guy who makes a living picking. Remember how fun it was. Sold that Schwinn to Jimmy Leffler for twenty bucks. Bought a bag of candy at Osco Drug and puked on your mom's carpet. I want to do that again."

"Puke on my mom's carpet?"

"No, moron. Make money selling rusty gold."

John gripped the side of my shoulder and stared into my eyes, "You have a wife and kid. Finding old bicycles and rusted out cars is not sustainable.

That was fun when we were kids. The days when our only responsibility was finding dirty magazines and making sure our parents didn't catch us spanking our monkeys. Those days are history. You need to grow up and provide for the family. I don't care what some old guy said."

"Not what he said. What I saw. He had barns full of rusty gold. He paid his mortgage with a rusty box."

John stared off into the distance and a smirk grew on his face. "We have to find jobs and pay bills," John said, rubbing his chubby cheek, "Sounds awful coming out of my mouth. I screwed up school and need to find *my* Plan B. I think the shop is a mistake."

I backed up to the street and held out my arms wide, "Look at this place. My entire life has been a mistake. No father. Living in small town Missouri with no options for a future. Unless you count working at the power plant and drinking beer at O'Malley's on Friday nights. Fell on my face in the military. I have a wife and young kid to take care of and drained my life savings and placed all my chips on the table of a dusty old butcher shop. What could go wrong? You in?"

John raised an eyebrow, "You want me to collect junk for a living? I don't think so. Too risky. If you recall, I just got kicked out of college and don't a have job. I'm staying at home with my mother's fifth husband, or boyfriend. Not sure. Risking my future on stealing bicycles and selling to kids is not wise at this juncture."

I shook my head, "After all these years, you're still a pussy and playing it safe. You will die alone and broke. Woman don't want a guy that always makes the rational decision."

"Let me know how Lisa takes your latest purchase. I'm willing to bet she won't be excited about your irrational decision. Can I have her number when she files for divorce?"

I slapped the empty Coke out of John's hand, "Go to hell. She trusts me. I'll just need to do some negotiating. It'll be practice for the new business."

"So, you in?"

"You still talking?"

"I'm serious. It will be like old times, my partner in crime."

"How much are you going to pay?"

I slipped my hands into my jeans, "Nothing... at first. I need to make a few sales before putting you on the payroll. Find a little part time job and help me on the side. When things pick up, you can be Vice President."

"Fine. But, I'm VP now. That's the only way I join this crazy ass business."

I reached a hand out to John, "Welcome aboard Mr. VP. I need to convince Lisa this is a good idea," I said, glancing up at the broken butcher sign, "Or I might live here."

10.

T he white full size Chevy van spit smoke from the back and backfired a couple times. I pressed on the mushy brakes and bumped the curb in front of John's house. He took a couple looks in the neighborhood to make sure no one saw the heap picking him up for a pick.

I lowered my sunglasses and tapped on the ripped leather of the steering wheel, "What you think? She's beautiful, right?"

John hesitated and yanked, with all his might, to open the passenger door. He slinked into the shredded seat, a spring poking his butt, "You didn't pay money for this, right? Tell me this was given to you by Uncle Hank. One of those cars he inherits when people can't pay their bill."

"Yes, Uncle Hank found it for me. But, no, I paid cash for it. Let's say I had to wheel and deal with Lisa."

John closed the door, "This will be good."

"Lisa wasn't happy about the business. I promised I'd talk with Uncle Hank about becoming a mechanic. She's convinced it'll flop. I needed a backup plan."

"How'd you end up with the van?" John asked, searching the glove box.

"Hank was excited about the new business and wanted to help. He showed me the van at his shop. Said it would be roomy enough for all the rusty gold we'd collect."

"You talk to Hank about becoming a mechanic?"

"Not exactly. He said it was a tough business. He told me to give the antique shop a try to see what happens. You only live once."

"Not going to tell Lisa?"

"Nope. Slept on the couch last night. Had to feed the kid all night with bottles."

"Told her about shop."

"Yep. Said something about the future of the family wouldn't depend on rusty signs and peoples junk. I wasn't listening too close. Isn't the van awesome?"

John read the owner's manual and smiled, "This thing is an '84. How many miles?"

I glanced at the odometer, "320,000. Uncle Hank said mostly highway miles, like new."

"Doubt it. The van is thirty years old."

"Mechanics know this kind of stuff."

John ignored my ignorance.

I handed John a slip of paper with an address on it, "Check it out."

"Whose address? Divorce attorney for when Lisa leaves you?"

"No, chubby. Our first pick. I met a guy who runs a dog farm. He said we could come and scour his collection."

"Dog farm? Is that the place my dad told me Snickers visited for the summer?"

"No, Snickers died. That's what dads say. This is one of those places where they breed puppies and save strays. We need to make money or I'm learning oil changes with Uncle Hank."

John slapped the dashboard and a plume of dust shot into the air, "Ain't no special farm for dogs in the country. Dad's a liar. Your piece of shit van ain't going to make it through the summer. Do you know how to make deals and buy peoples rusty gold?"

I slapped the steering wheel, "I negotiated this van. Only paid $400. Market value is at least $500," I said, giving a wink. John had a look on his face that said he wasn't convinced this van or the business had a future.

I didn't care. The rush of a new opportunity, despite the resistance and anger of Lisa, made all the difference, as we drove down the quiet highway of Missouri.

John pointed to an exit, waving the address in my face, "Turn left here."

The van bumped over the gravel road and slid along on bald tires, coughing like an old guy with a cigarette. I smiled, scanning the row of farms and houses popping up along the country road. I slapped John on the leg, "Isn't this awesome? We are doing it, man."

John nodded.

A long drive curved through a gravel road and a sign, hanging over the van, said Farmstead 51 in bright blue letters. I peeked and nodded at John. He was not amused.

"I'm going to see where Snickers is," he said, plopping down onto the dirt, and stretching his fat legs.

Half a dozen dogs, in a variety of breeds and sizes, came up to my leg and sniffed like I had a T-Bone strapped to my underwear. "Easy, boys. Where's your owner," I asked, as a short man with slicked back hair emerged from the house. He was waving like we'd been friends since school.

He led with a hand and looked at me and then at John, who was still trying to shake the stiffness out of his out of shape body. "I been expecting you boys. Don't mind the kids. They are harmless."

I looked around and, when I saw no kids, I realized he meant the dogs. Animal people can be weird.

"These are the newest of the litter. They can be hyper and jump on your leg. You show them a little force and they'll leave you alone. Tap their noses; that's what we do."

I nodded. "Thanks for the tip. We're looking for rusty gold. How can you help us?" I asked.

The small man pointed to a barn in the distance and handed me a key. "Unlock the barn. If you like anything inside, make me an offer. Simple."

I looked at the man and smiled and then looked back at John, not believing picking could be so easy. If every customer interaction went this smoothly, we'd be making money in no time and I'd be off the couch.

I snatched the key dangling from the hand of the owner and walked toward the barn. A Labrador ran in front of me and disappeared into the woods.

John wiped his nose. "Allergic to dogs. I remember why Snickers went to the farm. Dad two, or three, didn't want him in the house because my airway would swell up and I'd end up getting breathing treatments at the hospital. Been a while since I was around a dog," he said, giving out a weak cough.

"Don't let them rub on you. You'll be fine."

We arrived at the barn and I fiddled with the key. I was filled with nervous excitement over the potential of making money on our first official pick.

John helped me slide the heavy doors apart and waited to see the treasure inside.

The barn was full of rusty gold. Signs, cars, lamps, furniture, and tools, lots of rusty tools. I

winked at John and knew we were on to something.

11.

John hacked and spewed snot out of his nose in the corner of the barn. He waved telling me he needed to step outside and deal with the situation. I nodded as I examined a vintage lamp sure to be worth something good. Not mortgage payment good, but maybe a portion.

The barn was an eighty by eighty beauty filled to the rafters with rusty gold. I grinned and smiled and enjoyed the hunt for an item that would put Antique Adventures on the map. The business would succeed, regardless of what Lisa thought, or John, or the nagging self doubt in my head. My passion for rusty treasures and a stubborn will, not capable of quitting when times were tough, would ensure success.

I laid the lamp aside and reached for a Shell Oil sign of the 50's variety. I removed a layer of dust and stepped back to get a wide angle view of the vintage sign. This was a sign from the days of full service gas stations, beehive hairdos, and diners serving milkshakes for a dime. I set it aside, amongst a pile of other items I'd hoped to negotiate with the dog whisperer.

A bark in the front of the barn piqued my interest. I ignored the dog and climbed a ladder, opened a box on a high shelf, and pushed aside rusty junk to find better rusty junk.

I heard the bark a second time, but this time sounded like multiple dogs. John could be dead for all I knew, so I halted the search and checked on my snotty compadre.

John leaned over a wired mesh pen filled with barking pit bulls. These were not the dogs I'd imagine lying on your lap when watching a Chiefs football game. They were more of the saliva dripping and foaming at the mouth variety you'd see in *Cujo*.

I slapped John on the back. He startled, ignoring the dogs and wiping a green streak across his red cheeks, "I don't think playing with these dogs is helping the allergies," I said, scanning the snot stained shirt of John.

John wiped his nose, "Aren't they awesome? I couldn't help myself."

I looked around the yard, not wanting the owner to see John and me messing with the dogs. Afraid I'd ruin the pick, and he'd not want to sell. "If you're done playing with these monsters, please come back inside and help me with something. I found an old Shell Oil sign that might be worth looking at."

"Monsters? These dogs are sweet. Look at the way they jump up and down when I wave my hand over the pen."

The pit bulls leapt and snarled and spit flew from their jowls. They didn't have the look of playfulness; it was more I will eat out your heart if you mess with me.

"Not sure what you're looking at. But, these guys might be looking for dinner."

"Oh, come on, they're harmless. Let's open the pen and get a better look."

"Hell, no. I don't need no dog ripping out my neck. Besides, we need to make money and not scare a customer away by playing with *Cujo*."

John ignored my plea and fiddled with the metal latch on the pen. "I'm letting one out."

He unlatched the pen and three dogs rushed out and jumped on top of John who fell back on to the dirt. At first they licked his snot soaked cheeks, then the licking turned to nipping and their teeth showed.

A fourth dog ran up and growled and barked in my direction. I raised my hands and watched out of the side of my eye as John's dogs turned more aggressive.

"Bad idea, John. These dogs aren't looking to go on a walk."

The dog in front of me stood patient, with a

low rumbling growl, like he was thinking about his next move. I stood still and tried not to shit my pants. John's playful exuberance changed in to a high pitch plea.

"I don't want to play anymore," he said, snot now pouring from his nose and the spit of the dogs flinging onto his face.

"Should have thought about that before opening the damn pen. What do you suggest we do?"

John forearmed a couple dogs, as they continued to nip at his face, "You're the boss... You tell me."

The dog in front of me yapped and barked and lurched forward, nipping at my man parts. I stepped back, with each lurch, and kept an eye on John, making sure he wasn't being eaten for lunch.

"I have my Beretta. You want me to use it?"

John slapped a dog out of his face that was now getting aggressive, "Shoot em? No way. That would not be good for business. Maybe shoo them back into the pen. Why don't you yell for help?"

"One, I don't shoo saliva dripping dogs nipping at my crotch. I sure as hell ain't' yelling for the owner. Bad for business, too. When he saw your dumb ass opened the pen and let out his precious dogs, we'd be leaving empty handed. These monsters are probably sold to some gangsters in the city. He ain't going to think kindly about that."

The dog inched forward like we were in a dance, watching each other's moves. John was losing strength as he lay on his back and the other three dogs circled him.

A pit bull with a brown coat leapt at John and latched onto his forearm. He cried out and yelled for my help. I stood frozen, watching the dog shake his arm like an eagle with a squirrel in its mouth.

"I'm going to shoot now."

I kicked the dog in front of me, with my steel-toed boot, in his rib cage and he yelped and staggered back to the ground. My view was clear; I took a breath to calm the adrenaline and placed three quick bullets into the other three dogs jumping on John. The dogs fell over with a final chirp.

I felt a presence behind me and heard the scuffling of feet as the lone dog rushed me from behind. I heard a yelp as the dog careened to the side of me.

The owner stood over it like Muhammad Ali winning the world championship. "Bad dog. Leave these boys alone," he said, pointing at the dog. He cowered back like this wasn't the first time.

He peered around my body and glanced down to the ground where John laid with snot caked to his dirty face. The three dead dogs laid on their sides, scattered next to John.

The owner slowly walked to the dogs and knelt down listening to their chests.

"They're dead. What in the hell did you do?"

I jammed the Beretta back in my jeans and stammered and stuttered for words, "These monsters were attacking my friend. I was protecting him," I said, with confidence.

"These boys are not monsters. So you shot them? Why were they out of their cages?"

John waved from the ground, "My fault. I opened the pen to see if the dogs wanted to play. Was that a no-no?"

"Yes, asshole, a huge no-no. You hillbillies just flushed money down the drain. These pit bulls were sold to a customer. What am I supposed to tell them?"

"I'm sure you have other dogs available. These were not nice dogs. It's probably for the better," John said, looking over to one dead dog with its tongue hanging out.

"That's not the point, fatty. It is none of your business what these dogs *are*. I sold them to some guys in the city. It is their problem once they are sold."

"Gangsters?" John asked.

"What?"

"Never mind."

The man paced around the pile of dogs and scratched his head, "Who will pay for this?"

"I'm very sorry, sir. Why don't you come by the shop and get something nice for your farm. Store credit. I bet your wife would love something special," I said, forcing a plastic smile.

"I'm gay."

"Okay... maybe the boyfriend would like something."

"I don't have a boyfriend right now. You're going to pay for this. No store credit."

I paused and ran through the scenario in my head and realized we didn't have any items at the shop. The shop filled with piles of trash and construction supplies. We had to do some picking before opening the doors. Our inaugural pick was to fill the shop with items to sell. I was running low on cash, too.

"How much to replace these fine dogs?" I asked, opening my wallet.

"Fifteen hundred."

"Go to hell," I said, placing my wallet back in my jeans. "No way these monsters worth fifteen hundred. You can go to the local dog shelter and get one for $25," I said.

The man yanked a long blade from the side of his pants and waved it at us. "That's the price. You pay fifteen hundred or I cut you."

I yanked out the wallet and reluctantly paid the man.

He disappeared into the house. I looked at John and the dead dogs. "The old man was right. You needed protection. Picking is dangerous job," I said, glancing into my empty wallet, "And, we're broke."

John wiped his snot and didn't respond.

Let's say the first pick for Antique Adventures

was a bust. We were already down fifteen hundred. I was hoping Lisa would understand building a business takes time. If not, I was heading to community college.

12.

The Chevy van sputtered down the highway, making it difficult for conversation. John silent as he rubbed the cuts and scrapes on his forearms from the dogs.

"How's the Coke? Thought it might cheer you up," I said, the steering wheel vibrating from a crooked axel and the bald tires.

John stared out the cracked passenger window and sipped the Coke. He gave a pathetic nod, sipped the last drop, and placed the Styrofoam cup in the holder. "Thanks for saving me at the dog farm. Kind of freaked out right now."

I waved him off, "You'd do the same. Couldn't let those pit bulls eat you. They'd have enough food for a year," I said, pinching a wad of fat on his side.

John gave a weak smile but didn't want to play along with the fat joke. He turned back, with a stern look like he needed to use the can, "Not in the mood, Dex. Been thinking."

"That'll get you in trouble."

"I don't think the antique business is a good idea."

"Why? The dogs? A little fork in the road. We're fine. A learning lesson. The old man said be safe and come protected. I was, and we did. A couple scrapes will not stop Antique Adventures."

John examined the gouges in his arms and brushed his cut face, "We're not fine. I almost died. You're running out of money. Collecting rusty gold doesn't seem like a smart move in this season of life."

"You sound like my wife. Who knew you'd be the first one to bail."

John shoved his chewed up forearm in my face, "Things could get worse. Next time dead and buried in some barn in the backwoods of Missouri."

"So?"

"So? You got a wife and kid. I'm in between relationships but hope to get a lady someday. I don't want to be one of those stories on the news where they find our bodies buried in a freezer somewhere. You don't always have to be a hero, Dex."

I waved off John and was getting upset. The top of my head getting warm. "I ain't trying to be no hero. Just trying to provide a life for my family. Maybe a life that's not confined to the expectations of the people in LeClaire. I don't want to look back when I'm old and regret playing it safe and choosing the easy road. What you so scared about? The dog guy? He had his issues, yes, I'll give you that. But, that was an isolated incident. The old man taught me the ropes, and he makes a shit ton of money. I want some of it. We got to give it time. Besides, your big ass body ain't going to fit in a freezer," I said, with a wink, hoping to change John's resistance to acceptance.

John shook his head and popped the top off the empty Coke and chewed on the ice. "Don't know if I'm cut out for the rusty gold business. This is your thing, not mine. What's the big deal if I bail? Find another partner."

I became animated and played back laying down those four dogs, "John, you're my Robin. Batman needs his partner, or it's not the same. Admit killing those dogs was fun. There was something freeing about protecting you from becoming a meat sandwich."

John raised an eyebrow, "You enjoyed killing those dogs? You're sick."

"No, not like that. It wasn't the dogs. Feeling of saving a life. When I signed up for the SEALS, I wanted to protect people. After being sent home, I still felt like I needed to be a protector. You know what I mean?"

"Not sure, but you are hell of a shot. You laid down those drooling pit bulls in quick fashion."

I nodded a couple times, liked affirmation from John, "One of the SEALS instructors said I was one of the best shots they'd seen. Got to use the skills for something, right?"

"You're not a killer. We are pickers. If this business has a chance for survival, we have got to stay focused on the task at hand. Making money."

I held out a pinky, "I pinky swear only to use a gun if you're being attacked by dogs. Any other predator, you are on your own," I said, with a smile.

"I still don't know, Dex. My head says no about the business, and my heart says yes. Because you are my best friend, and I have no prospects on the horizon."

"How's the part time gig at Rudy's?"

"I keep getting yelled at for drinking out of the milkshake machine."

"You're a disgusting human."

"Had their shakes? Unreal."

I didn't answer.

"We're getting our first sales so you can quit the part time gig. You need no more unnecessary calories."

John gazed into the distance as the Missouri highway flew by the window. "Did you hear me?" I asked.

"Sorry, thinking about milkshakes."

"Idiot."

We pulled the van in front of Antique Adventures and it sputtered off. I unlocked the front door and scoped out the inside of the shop. Ladders, paint buckets, and mismatched furniture strewn around on the inside.

"Looks empty," John said.

I framed my fingers and looked in between, "You need to imagine what it could be. Shelves in every corner, stacked with rusty gold. A nice counter with cabinets full of treasures making us boat loads of money. See it?"

John knelt on the ground and glanced back at me, "How about floors without holes?"

"That's nothing. Antique Adventures will be a booming business, you watch. With me?"

John shrugged.

A phone tethered to the wall rang. I scurried over and flung the receiver in the air, "See, first customer..." I said, giving John a tongue, "Antique Adventures. One man's junk, another man's treasure, how can I help you today?"

I listened to the woman drone on with details regarding the call. I nodded and tried to stay interested. She left an eight hundred number.

"Someone wants to buy an antique we don't have?" John asked, examining the empty store.

I yanked out my wallet and opened the bill compartment to an empty void. "How much money you got?" I asked John.

John opened his wallet, "Couple bucks, why?"

"Mortgage company called. I gave my last fifteen

hundred to the dog guy. We're late on our pay-ments."

13.

5 *years later...*
I banged my head on the desk as I poured over a spreadsheet with the latest numbers from Antique Adventures. The numbers were dipping like John's man boobs at the pool. In 2008, an economic crash had made people tighten their wallets. They didn't see rusty gold to adorn their suburban homes as a necessity. I get it, but it sucked for business.

Lisa came into our home office with her hair in a bun, wearing tight jeans and a short Nirvana t-shirt. I pulled her in and kissed her soft legs, "Need some sugar. Numbers are not good. The ship is leaking oil and going down," I said, glancing up and giving Lisa pouty eyes, hoping for sympathy.

She ripped the document from the desk and examined the numbers, "It can't be that bad. We've been here before," Lisa said, pointing to a line item, "Spending way too much on advertising. Antique

Adventures is a word-of-mouth business. Website, phone book listings, and print materials are a waste of money," she said, tossing the spreadsheet back on the desk.

"How'd you get so smart in business?" I said, hugging her waist.

She popped out a hip, "Made the same mistake at the Power Plant. Dumped a bunch of advertising dollars for a quick buck. Instead of thinking long term and for the good of the community, we went for a cash grab. That why I don't work there anymore, me and hundreds of other people in LeClaire."

Lisa was right. She worked for the Power Plant for five years before being laid off when the facility closed. It was a big hit on LeClaire and I saw the effects staring back at me in the latest revenue numbers.

"Cut advertising, check. What else can we do, smarty pants? I'll be going back to community college and looking for a new line of work."

"First, you should've listened five years ago and never started the business," she said, sticking out a tongue, "Second, you can still become a mechanic. Uncle Hank's retiring soon and needs someone to take over the shop."

I banged my head on the desk, "We still talking about this? Honey, I'm no mechanic, and that ship has sailed. We need to turn around Antique

Adventures. Had a good first five years considering the economy, right?"

Lisa leaned down and wrapped her soft arms around my neck and kissed my head, "Sorry, that wasn't nice. You allowed me to stay home with Spencer. You can't put a price on that..." she said.

A blonde haired five-year-old burst into the office holding a small device, "Hi, dad. You got any batteries? My *Toy Story* game is not working," Spencer said, revealing his dimples and freckled cheeks.

I reached into the top drawer of the metal desk and slid open the door, "Double A or Triple A?" I asked.

"The big ones," Spencer said, holding out a hand no larger than the batteries.

"Double As it is," I said, kissing Spencer on the head.

I hunched down to eye level, "Can you tell mommy why Antique Adventures is awesome? How daddy loves his job and wants to give it to his son when he's old enough to buy his own batteries."

Lisa wagged her finger, "Passive aggressive, you think? I'm standing right here."

"What's passive aggressive?" Spencer asked.

We both laughed.

I kissed him again and sent him out of the room. "I'll explain it later. You play with Buzz Lightyear and let us finish our conversation."

Spencer pranced out of the office, staring at the game, and never looked up.

"If I don't want to take over Hank's shop, Plan B?"

"You need to cut back. Find any and every possible way to save money."

"I'm already running lean. The only big expense I can cut is John's salary."

Lisa shrugged.

"Hell no. He's my best bud and has a lot invested in the business. John will work at Rudy's again. And the milkshake machine and he doesn't mesh."

Lisa understood John, and I were best friends and he depended on work from AA. He took a huge risk joining the team and to fire him would devastate him. He would never find a job in LeClaire that paid well.

"I get it. If you can't cut John... simple business principle, you need more revenue. Make more money than you spend, a lot more, and you'll keep AA's doors open."

"Thank you, Captain obvious. We need help to find more picking spots. We've milked every rusty barn, garage, and house dry, in Missouri and parts of Kansas. How do we find places in Iowa and Nebraska? I heard there are opportunities outside Des Moines and Lincoln."

"It'll cost you. Gas, food, hotels, and wear and tear on the van. How about those spots in southern

Missouri? Outside Carthage? You and John haven't done much work there."

I leaned back in the swivel chair and stared at the numbers on the revenue sheet. A pit grew in my stomach knowing AA was leaking oil and my business acumen had hit a wall. I was the cowboy scraping by on charm, decent negotiating skills, and love for the next adventure. My business IQ was not my strong suit, at this point. Maybe I needed to consider doing an apprenticeship under Uncle Hank and call it a day.

The phone rang.

"Yes, this is Dexter," I said, responding to the robotic tone on the other line.

I hung my head and glanced at Lisa, who could tell unsettled by the call. She whispered, "Who is it?"

I didn't answer and hung my head over the papers spilled on the desk. "Okay, I'll see what I can do, thank you," I said, hanging up the phone and slamming my fist into the papers spewing them across the office.

"What?" Lisa asked, "Look like you saw a ghost."

"Worse, credit card company. We're officially maxed out. They need a minimum payment or will take legal action."

Lisa backhanded me and huffed, "Shit, Dex. How in the hell did that happen? You spending money the business doesn't have?"

"I spent money on the website and some phone book ads. But, they ain't making the shop any money. I didn't have the cash."

"What are you going to do? The bank won't give you a loan. You have already used all lines of credit."

I sighed and felt the top of my head warm with anger and confusion. The thing I wanted so badly was slipping through my broke fingers. "Can we get a loan from your folks?"

Lisa hit me again, "Remember how we bought this house?"

"Good point. What do we do? Tell me. I need someone to make the next decision. I got nothing left," I said, laying my head on the desk.

"Call it a day."

"Excuse me."

"Close down the shop. You tried, and it's not working. I want you to sell it, pay off our debts, and move on. Call my uncle and get a job at the shop. No shame in this, Dex," Lisa said, caressing my messy black hair.

I rose to my feet and pointed at Lisa, "You'd like that wouldn't you? Crush my dreams once again. It's always about you and your damn family. Working for Uncle Hank is all that matters. You don't care I don't know shit about cars. I'm doing what I love and you want to rip out my heart and stomp on it. No way we quit this easy."

Lisa stayed calm and fought back a tear. I

couldn't tell if she wanted to cry or punch me in the head. "Crush your dreams, huh? You think I want to destroy your life? If we're being honest, who's the one who started this business without asking me? Who dumped their entire life savings into collecting rusty gold with no backup plan? If anyone is selfish, look in the mirror. That's not fair. I break my back taking care of you and Spencer. How dare you put this on me?"

I reached out a hand and Lisa recoiled, "Sorry, baby. We're in a tough spot. You do a ton for the family. We can figure it out. Too much invested into this business to quit now. I know we can get over the hump and make this thing viable."

Lisa chewed on her nails and tapped her toes, contemplating a response, "The choice is the family, or the business. What do you want?"

I was caught off guard. Didn't like the options as nothing in me wanted to pull the plug on the business. I was getting in my groove and learning how to negotiate and find good items for the shop. Not the best business mind, but I was rolling up my sleeves and making it happen. If we could navigate a rocky economy, our future would be bright.

"Don't make me choose, that's not fair."

"Choose, Dexter, or get out."

I ended up on the couch at John's house.

14.

"Pull."

John yanked on the string and the clay pigeon flew into the air as I stared down the target. I followed the fake bird to the right and let it come down a few feet and pulled the trigger on the rifle.

The clay exploded, a plume of smoke surrounding the nonexistent remnant of a bird. "Felt good."

"You're hot today. SEALS training made you a better shot. All that anger channeled on those little birdies, I guess," John said, with a smile, still staring out to the empty field in the back of his mother's house.

"Something like that," I said, lost in the euphoria of watching the bird explode.

"She kicked you out, huh?" John said.

"Cause of you," I said, winking at John and realigning the rifle, "Pull."

John launched another pigeon into the sky. I

exploded it out of the sky. A hawk took off in the distance and cried out.

John scratched his head, "My fault... How so?"

"Lisa wanted me to fire you. I told her hell no, and she kicked me out. There might've been other things said, too."

John stuck his rifle in the dirt and pointed to the wide open piece of Missouri land, "The ladies are a mystery. They say there's more fish in the sea. I've been fishing a long time and the line ain't got no pull. You tracking?"

I adjusted my John Deere hat and wiped sweat from my forehead, "Confused as hell."

"Let me use laymen terms. You always choose your lady. Pain in the ass sometimes. But, life without them ain't worth living," John said, turning back to his mother's house, "I think about it daily in my childhood bed."

I nodded. "Got it. You saying I should of chose Lisa and Spencer and not the business?"

"Yes, sir. That should've been an easy choice."

I slumped onto a bench behind the makeshift shooting range and sipped on a Coors, "It should be easy. Hot wife, the funniest kid. Something's wrong with me, John. Why choosing the family over the business or the next adventure is so damn hard. I'd do anything for them and still I can't make the right decisions. Got like this restless soul that doesn't stay quiet. Help me, bro."

John nodded and rubbed his chin like a wise sage

ready to say something profound, "You know what I'd do?"

"Tell me."

He slapped me in the side of my head, the beer spilling in my lap. "What the hell? Spilled my beer. You're paying for the next twelve."

"You stupid, Dex? The business is not important right now. Family is all we got, and, even my whore mother, with her many husbands, is all I got. We don't get many shots at keeping the family together. When life is falling apart, they are the safety net. Go home and beg and plead and tell Lisa and Spencer you love them. Do the right thing."

I tossed the empty beer can into the dirt, "I love them. More than life. I don't want to lose the business. Don't want to lose my family, either. It's like every time I have to choose between family and the business. Why can't I have both? Without AA there ain't no house or shoes for the kid, and we're eating Sloppy Joe's out of a can. Lisa's always pressuring me to ignore the business and pay more attention to the family. I don't see it like that. Paying attention to AA is so I can give more attention to them. Get it?"

John smiled and glanced up from his beer, "Can I ask Lisa out if you divorce? She's cute."

"You're not listening to a damn word I say. She ain't into chubby guys, anyway. Likes em lean and mean like me," I said, lifting my T-shirt and showing off my six pack to John.

"You keep drinking those beers and you'll catch up. SEALS training was a long time ago."

I waved off John and thought about the SEALS and the business and failing at life, "Those were good days. Damn knee cost me something of significance. Why I can't be happy. Looking for the next battle to fight and hill to climb. I would've of been a great SEAL. Swam circles round those guys," I said, staring off into the distance.

"Swim back into the present. You got a family that needs their husband and daddy. Forget about the next adventure. Think about what's in front of you. The one regret every man faces at the end of the line is not how much money they made or their work success. They regret not spending time with the ones they loved."

I nodded and leaned back on the bench and enjoyed the gentle summer breeze brushing my warm face. I lowered my hat over my eyes, "You read that in Reader's Digest? Gonna rest my eyes a second and maybe discover this was all a bad dream."

I settled on to the bench and sleep flooded my tired body. My phone lit up in my pocket, jolting me awake. I didn't recognize the number and caught it before they hung up, "Dexter, here."

I nodded and John could see the seriousness on my face. He elbowed me in the side, "Creditor?"

I held up a finger and covered my other ear, trying to focus on the words from the woman on the other line. She sounded serious and like she was hiding something.

"You sure? Lisa and Spencer O'Kane? I'll come right down."

I looked at the phone like it had two heads and was winking back at me. The hawk circled over head and I caught a glimpse and glanced back at John.

"Everything all right?" John asked.

"Lisa and Spencer were in an accident. They're at the hospital."

15.

W e jumped into the Antique Adventures van as it sputtered down the road, I wasn't sure of two things. One, if the van would make it to the hospital in one piece, and two, if my family would be okay. The nurse, on the phone, had been vague, and I didn't know what the hell I was walking into.

John reached out a hand of comfort, "It will be okay, Dex. Your family is strong. Don't go to a bad place until we have the details."

I wiped a tear from my face and gripped the steering wheel almost ripping it from the column, "I can't deal right now. This is too much. How in the hell could I even consider a damn business over my flesh and blood? What's wrong with me?"

"Don't go there. That doesn't matter. Just get to the hospital."

The van sputtered and backfired in front of LeClaire Regional Hospital, the only medical facility in the area. An orderly pushing an older woman in wheelchair gave a grin and a head shake, knowing the van was a piece of shit.

"Where's the ER?" I yelled at the orderly, forgetting the van was running. I raced back, shut it down, and waited for a response.

"You can't leave that there?" the man said, pointing to the van.

I tossed him the keys, "Keep it. Where's the ER?"

The keys flew by his head and he didn't make an attempt at a catch. "Sir, you can't leave that there. Security will tow it."

"Tow it. It's worth less than my jeans. Where's the ER, dick?"

The old woman in the wheelchair lit up with a smile. He pointed to the right, "Enter the sliding doors and hang a right."

I waved John over and we entered the hospital, hung a right, and two automatic doors raced open. The ER filled with nurses, doctors, and patients moaning with pain. I scanned the room and saw a front desk.

"Need the room of Lisa and Spencer O'Kane. Where are they?" I said, the room blurring, and I realized I had eaten nothing. Not to mention the stress was weighing on my mind and focus.

A tall, slender man nudged in on my conversation with the nurse at the counter. "You, Mr. O'Kane? Family of Lisa and Spencer?" he asked, with a stern look on his clean shaven face.

"Mr. O'Kane is my father. Dexter... I'm husband

and father. Father and husband, whatever," I said, grabbing my head, and trying to stop my brain from spinning like a Ferris wheel.

"Do you need to sit down, sir?" the doctor asked, grabbing my shoulder as my knees buckled.

John and the doctor carried me across from the desk to a bank of chairs and settled me in. The doctor glanced at a clipboard and back at me, "This is hard to say. Lisa and Spencer came in with multiple injuries."

I heard the voice of the doctor but it wasn't computing and people were talking around me and I couldn't focus on the reality of the moment.

I mustered words I wasn't sure made any sense, "What happened?"

"They were in a serious car accident. The police found them off the highway, up against a tree."

"How is that possible? I just saw them a couple days ago."

"A couple days ago?" the doctor asked, lowering his thin rimmed glasses.

"A long story."

"This is a confusing time. No one ever imagines having to deal with the loss of a loved one."

"A loss? What, are they alive?"

The doctor leaned in and massaged my shoulder, "They are alive. We did everything we could. But, they need help breathing. Lisa and Spencer are on life support machines."

I stared at the floor and then back at the doctor

and John, I didn't want to receive the words he said. I placed my head in my hands and felt the room get dark.

I collapsed to the floor.

The doctor called a nurse over who gave me a juice and a cold cloth for my head. I glanced to the doctor who was talking and I couldn't translate his words. The lips were moving and nothing was computing in my head.

"What happened? I thought you told me my family was on life support. Where am I?"

The doctor forced a grin, "You passed out for a few seconds. I think you need sugar and food. It is a lot to take in right now. Dexter, you will need to make a big decision. The quality of life for Lisa and Spencer is not good."

I sipped on the juice and raised an eyebrow. "What kind of decision?"

"They are not breathing on their own. Brain activity is minimal. They are both in a coma because their brains are swelling. We don't think they will make it through the night. I'm so sorry..." the doctor said, placing a cold hand on my thigh.

I rose from the chair and threw the cup of juice into the middle of the busy hallway. The workers and patient's heads turned toward me, "I can't do this shit. My business is falling apart. My family is on machines. I didn't say I was sorry... it can't end like this..."

The doctor and John sat back in their chairs and

gave me a second to rant. John came up and said nothing. He wrapped his arms around me and I could hear him choke up. "Lisa and Spencer were lucky to have you in their lives. Hang on to that... buddy. This isn't your fault. It was an accident."

The doctor came over, after the moment with John, and whispered in my ear. "Why don't we go see your family?"

I didn't answer and John forced me to follow the doctor and kept his bear arms over my body. We opened the door to their room and the sound of beeping machines. A device chirped, raising up and down, helping them breathe.

Spencer's head covered in a bandage that looked like a turban. Lisa looked the same. A tube jammed down each of their throats. There was blood and cuts on their swollen faces. The quiet and darkness of the room placed a pit in my stomach.

The doctor pointed to an open area between their beds. He said, "Take your time. I'll be in the hall."

John left with the doctor.

I dropped to my knees in between the beds and stared at the ceiling. My mind cluttered with the sounds of life support machines and regret. Not sure if this was real or a dream. I looked to heaven, "Oh, God. I'm sorry. If this is punishment, I get it. My family was never first priority. I'm selfish and only thought about the next adventure and the business," I said, wiping tears from my warm face,

Ryan J. Pelton

"But, God, if you have one more miracle left in the arsenal, I need one now."

I reached and grabbed each of their hands on the sides of the beds. Looked at Lisa first, "I love you baby. There is nothing I wouldn't do for you. I'm sorry for being a selfish ass. You've been my world since high school. Please forgive me. I chose the business over you and Spencer. If you wake up, things will be different. I promise…"

I wiped my nose and shifted to Spencer, "Son… you are the best thing that ever happened to this selfish man. Reading books before bed, Lego on the floor, and teaching you how to shoot a gun in the woods. Don't tell mom," I said, smiling at Lisa, "I always wanted to be the dad I never had. But, I failed. The business took up a lot of time. I tried to be present and, the picking game called me away. I'm sorry, son. When you wake up, things will be different. I will never choose the business over you… I swear."

I rose from the floor and kissed each of them on the cheek. Their faces were cold and lifeless.

I stood at the door before entering the hallway and a movie played of my wedding day and the day I met Spencer. Tears were streaming down my face and soaking the floor.

I had a meeting with the doctor and a couple other medical professionals to decide their fate. The hardest decision any human could ever have to make. Not a choice of whether you make business or family a priority. A choice of whether someone lives or dies.

We pulled the plug. The trauma to Lisa and Spencer was too severe for any quality of life beyond a week. For what it's worth it brought peace to the situation.

I now suffer alone. It was the last time I'd ever see my family on earth. The prayer for a miracle wasn't answered. I have a business but I don't have them.

I'm not sure if the tradeoff was equal.

Sneak Peek: Hired Gun (Antique Assassin Book 1)

What happened to Dexter after the death of Lisa and Spencer? Was the car accident really an accident? Here is the first chapter of *Reborn* which continues the timeline of the Antique Assassin and Dexter O'Kane crime adventures.

You can get *Hired Gun* where books are sold.

Chapter 1

Death and rain mingled together.

Drops of water bounced off a sea of black umbrellas that shot upward like skyscrapers. I shifted in my uncomfortable wooden chair, surrounded by hundreds of people listening to the pastor on the outdoor lawn.

A large, black casket, perched like a gargoyle, hovered over its eventual home: a silent hole waiting to embrace her victims.

Next to the larger one, a smaller box elbowed in—a size reserved for premature death. I looked up hard, trying to fight off tears.

The echoing of the pastor's voice was muted by small outbursts of weeping as the death boxes lowered into the ground. Outside, shells. Inside, souls. The hope of a merger in heaven.

I scratched my unshaven face, shifted to the side, and felt the wood stabbing my lower back. A five-o'clock-shadow was a reminder of two truths: I hate shaving most days, and when your family dies, it is not a high priority.

The flood of emotion choked my insides, hitting me like a truck plowing through a deer on the highway. I tried to breathe in normal time with little luck.

I bowed my head.

Tears dripped onto the grass, keeping time with the pounding rain.

My church shoes, reserved for Christmas, Easter, and an occasional funeral, were soaked with water and sadness.

Why, God? I breathed through the tears.

A large, warm arm wrapped around my slouching shoulders. "I'm sorry, brother. It's not right," John said, stroking the back of my black suit.

John Wood is my best friend. Partner in crime from life's first breath. The Wood and O'Kane families lived close together for most of their existence in LeClaire, Missouri. A small, blue-collar town, spattered with a few immigrants—my family included.

The O'Kanes emigrated from Ireland when my grandparents determined the lack of jobs would be a problem. They came to America in the 50's, looking for the American Dream. They found their slice of the pie in LeClaire.

My grandfather, a meat man—butcher, to be correct—operated a store on the corner of Main and Green. He worked hard, serving the people of LeClaire with beef, pork, and sausage. Many tables in our town were adorned with a sticker reading "The Local Pig".

I stared at my tear-stained hands and peered into John's bloodshot eyes. "Did I do something wrong? Why is this happening?" I said, leaning back in the wooden folding chair.

John's large hand swallowed mine. "Oh, man, don't even go there. You were a great husband and the best dad. Lisa and Spencer were fortunate to have you in their lives."

I loved Lisa more than life, like take-a-bullet, my-heart-hurts kind of love. The obsession originated at a high school basketball game. The LeClaire

Bulldogs were playing our cross-town rival, the Greeley Gators. I didn't play basketball because uncoordinated Irish kids named Dexter didn't make the NBA. So I cheered from the stands.

Lisa danced across the gym floor, cheering on our school. She was the cheerleader and I the non-jock. Her long, blond hair bounced off her red and white skirt. I knew Lisa was the mythical One before she did.

We dated senior year and married the following summer. No reason to wait. Couples married young in small towns. In LeClaire, people view marriage and childbearing with different lenses compared to city folk. Having enough money or traveling to Europe before marriage is not considered in our town. Life begins and ends in LeClaire for her twenty thousand residents.

Spencer was born four years later. The happiest time of my life. A half-Irish, half-German grew and developed his own personality, and I hoped he would have more of the German side, and less of the too-much-drinking Irish side.

I promised a stable home to my family. My father left for prison when I was six. That's a story for another day.

The sounds of timpans, fifes, and bagpipes played *Be Thou My Vision*. A song played at our wedding. Nothing pierced deeper than authentic Irish folk music. When the bagpipes came out, it was celebration or death. No middle ground.

My father emigrated with his family from Ireland on his first birthday. He lived across the street from my mother and stalked her early. I wished he had used his tenacity for the common good.

I whispered in John's ear, "I need a drink. You want to head over to O'Malley's?"

John lurched forward as if being stung by a bee. "O'Kane, you can't leave. Can't a beer wait? Your family needs you, man."

My black tie pinched the life out of my thick Irish neck, and I gave it a tug. John peered at me, I gave a *let's get out of here* stare and nod. "I don't have a family; they're buried in the ground. O'Malley's for Happy Hour if you want a ride."

I slid out of the chair, used an umbrella to shield my identity, and moved like a cat burglar trying to escape the bagpipes, tears, and sadness. My head dropped and I tried not to make eye contact with any mourners as the rain intensified.

My tears stopped.

I walked through rows of gravestones, tapping them with my hand, counting the years between the lines.

Death is not fair.

From behind a tree a man appeared, wearing a black trench coat and holding an umbrella. I gave a half smile, and tried weaving to the left, and he stopped me in the center.

"Excuse me, pal. I'm just trying to get to the car," I said.

"This was no accident," the man said.

"What did you say?"

"These deaths were no accident," he said.

I pushed the man's right shoulder out of the way. "You don't know what you're talking about. I need to get to the car, psycho," I said.

He relented, and moved to the side.

I kept walking toward the car, rain falling, I looked back one more time.

The man disappeared behind a tree. I scanned the cemetery and browsed the green, wet landscape.

Gone.

I drank alone at O'Malley's.

Sneak Peek: Stranger Danger (Antique Assassin Book 2)

Why did Dexter grow up without a dad? What happens when he comes home after thirty years of prison? Trouble of course... Here is the first chapter of *Return* which continues the Antique Assassin and Dexter O'Kane crime adventure series.

You can get *Stranger Danger* where books are sold.

Chapter 1

The black truck reversed and the sound of squealing tires echoed in the chamber of my ringing ears. Glass covered our bodies as I lay over my father. A jagged piece leaned against my sweaty neck.

I peeked up above the now missing back window and listened for more action.

Nothing.

I whispered in my dad's ear, "You okay?"

No response.

I cleared away a path of broken chards of glass from his neck and placed two fingers over his wrinkled skin.

Heart still beating.

I sat up and glanced out the front of the truck and caught the black vehicle driving at the right side of the parking lot. A debris and dust cloud lifted from behind the speeding vehicle.

I fired up the engine and placed a hand on my father's back. I could feel his skinny ribs moving with bated breath. He moaned, squirmed, and went silent in the passenger seat.

I reached behind the seat in the extended cab and pulled out a black duffel. A Beretta .92FS pistol stared back at me. I yanked on the magazine release button to check ammunition. Full. I laid the black beauty on my lap and gassed the truck.

The truck rumbled and glass danced up and down in the cab. I gave my father a couple looks to check for progress. My truck gained ground on the speeding black vehicle. I placed the gun in my left hand, pulled down my sunglasses with the right, and took aim at the back window of the vehicle.

One. Miss. Two. Miss. Third. Hit.

The vehicle swerved to the left, right, and straight on the two-lane road. I glanced at the rearview mirror to see the prison getting smaller in the distance. A swarm of oak trees hung over the road as our loud vehicles raced down the highway.

I gained on the small pickup truck and hit the brakes as it veered to the left and smashed into a large tree. The front of the radiator spewed water and steam. My truck fishtailed, and I yanked it back to center just past the mangled car. I pulled back around to eye the driver.

The driver kissed the steering wheel and blood rushed down the center of his forehead. I scanned both sides of the road looking for any passersby.

Quiet.

I pressed my face into the arm of my hoodie trying to shield the smell of smoke. The front end of the truck looked like an accordion and fluids squirted from every orifice of the vehicle.

I wiggled the handle of the truck door and reached in for the body. He was still. Blood poured down the middle of his face from a wound in his hairline. The man, dark-skinned, brown hair, and wearing a yellow hoodie. Not much older than twenty-five.

The truck smoked and sizzled from the engine compartment and out of the dashboard.

I wrapped my arms under his armpits, drug the body around the passenger side of the vehicle, and laid him on a soft patch of grass and leaves near a ditch. I stood over the body for a moment to get a better look. No match in my brain.

I checked both sides of the road, sprinted back to my truck, and set my Beretta on the center console. I grabbed the gun and poked my father. "You alive?"

He was now making noise and moaning, awakening from his short sleep. "I thought two people would die today."

My father moaned, and his eyes fluttered, as I sped past the burning vehicle. I watched the truck in the rearview ignite in flames as we fled.

My father fluttered his eyes and raised his head from his short sleep. He looked down at the tags of glass clinging to his Member's Only jacket. "What happened? You okay, son?" he said, looking me over.

"Everything's fine now. We had a situation after the prison visit."

My father scanned the surrounding wooded road from the passenger window and picked glass from his bloody arm. "Did everything go okay at the prison? Did they harass you?"

"Not exactly. But, not a good day for the man in the yellow hoodie."

"Who? Is he a guard?"

I placed my hand on my father's leg picking out

a shard of glass. "It doesn't matter. Why don't you take a nap? We have a long ride to LeClaire."

"Where's LeClaire?"

I pressed the gas, and the truck worked hard down the Kansas highway. "It's in Missouri. My home. Maybe your home, depending on how you behave," I said, with a grin.

Sneak Peek: Color Blind (Antique Assassin Book 3)

When a racist group called American Renaissance comes to LeClaire. Dexter and John are in deep. Will they stop this evil group before they brainwash more people to join their agenda? With lots of action and laughs... You know you're in for a Missouri thrill ride!

Here is the first chapter of *Revenge* which continues the Antique Assassin and Dexter O'Kane crime adventure series.

You can get *Color Blind* where books are sold.

Chapter 1

Nelson Darby held his arm steady, staring down the long black barrel. A car rushed in front of his eyes and he backed off to reset.

Really?

He sighed, steadied himself, and turned his baseball cap around, while snapping a lucky piece of gum. Trident.

The double lane street was busy with the normal lunchtime traffic in downtown LeClaire, Missouri. The restaurants were filled with a mixture of day laborers and white and blue collar workers, white, black, young and old.

Nelson locked in on a handsome African American couple sipping Iced Tea and gazing deep into each other's eyes. Married? Dating? Brother and sister? Who knows?

He twisted the barrel slightly to the right and back to the left. Squinting his eye, he took one last breath before pulling the trigger.

Click.

He pulled the Canon SLR1 back and examined the small LCD screen. Nelson pressed a button on top of the camera and waited for it to change.

Looked like a winner.

Nelson unscrewed the long lens and packed it in a black carrying case. He edged to the curb, checked both ways for traffic, spit out the gum, and galloped across the street.

The young black couple, of about twenty, with

faces immersed in salads, sandwiches, and each other, were oblivious to the scrawny white man standing at the edge of their table.

Nelson stuck out a hand, "Sorry to bother you in the middle of lunch. Do you have a second?" he asked, adjusting the camera bag wrapped around his shoulder.

A strong, wide-chested man peeked up from his salad, annoyed by the interruption. His good looking companion, sitting across the round patio table, squirmed in her seat, wiped the remnants of a Turkey Club from her lip, and gripped his hand across the table.

"We're trying to eat lunch. What's this about?" the man asked.

Nelson's hand dangled over the middle of the table; he pulled it back, and continued his spiel, "Name's Nelson and I'm a photography student at LeClaire Community College. Been photographing an eagle perched above the top of the restaurant and you beautiful people caught my eye," Nelson said, pointing to a Maple tree hovering over the sign: All Seasons Cafe.

The black man raised a brow and glanced at the woman. "Okay... what do you want?"

"Well, I, ugh, took a couple pics of you eating lunch. That okay?" Nelson asked, as he jammed his hands into his jean pockets, trying to keep the camera bag steady on his shoulder.

"Why are you taking pictures of us? Never seen

black folks in LeClaire before? Rare as that eagle you were photographing," the man said with a grin, looking for confirmation from his girlfriend.

Nelson gave an awkward half-smile as his face turned red. He shuffled his Converse on the hot cement, "You're black? Didn't notice. My momma taught us to be colorblind. Wasn't it Martin Luther King who said it's not the color of the skin, but...."

The man held up a hand. "Stop before you embarrass yourself. Got it. You're not a racist," he said, taking a sip of Iced Tea.

Nelson swung his camera bag off his shoulder and flipped open a large compartment in the top. He yanked out a small business card and handed one to the couple. A car honked behind him causing him to lurch.

"Like I said, I was trying to shoot a rare eagle in Missouri. Never seen one in the city..."

The man examined the card and looked back at Nelson. "How does this concern us?" he asked.

"I'm looking for models to help with a website design and marketing project for class. You're a beautiful couple and just what I need. Interested?" Nelson asked with a toothy grin.

The black man cleared his throat, "I'm guessing you need a token black couple for the project. Appear inclusive and diverse. Is that what this is all about?" he asked, watching as his girlfriend shook her head.

"Oh no, sir. I think you two have impeccable

features and could make serious money with your flawless faces. And, help a starving artist," Nelson said, closing the camera bag.

The woman examined the card and smiled. "You think we have impeccable features? Few famous models come out of LeClaire," she said.

"Few famous people period. I think the most famous was the guy who won American Idol, David something," Nelson said.

They both laughed.

"This sounds fishy. But, what if we were interested? Is there an audition or something?" the man asked, wiping a bead of sweat from his perfect complexion.

Nelson leaned over the table and pointed at the business card. "No audition. Seen everything I need. All you need to do is visit the website, key in the password, and you'll see some of my past work. If you think this is something that might interest you, call the number at the bottom. I'll take care of the rest," he said as he stepped away from the table and dodged a man riding a bike down the sidewalk.

The couple looked at one another and then back at Nelson.

Nelson said, "No pressure. Not every day you run into such beautiful people. I want to capture this moment. I think we could be on to something good for everyone."

The woman batted her long eyelashes and placed her hand on her boyfriend. "Come on honey. Let's check out the website. What's the harm?" she asked.

He examined the card and then glanced up at Nelson. "All right. We'll check it out. Can we please finish the rest of our lunch?" he asked, peeking at a wristwatch.

Nelson held up his hands in supplication. "Thanks for allowing me to interrupt your lunch. You will not regret checking out the website. I think you'll like my work. Maybe you'll be the next famous people from LeClaire. Like the American Idol guy..."

The couple looked at each other and smiled.

Nelson glided back across the street and unlocked the door to an older Honda Civic. He fiddled with his camera bag, pulled out the Canon, and rolled down the window. He aimed it through the opening.

One more photo of these beautiful people. A people that deserved to be wiped from the earth.

How to make an author crazy grateful

If you liked this book, and want to see more in the series, I can help. And, there are some things you can do that will help me out a ton:

(1) **Review this Book**

Go to wherever you purchased this title, and leave an honest review. You have no idea how that helps me keep writing and publishing. I want to build a rabid tribe of fans that want more of my stuff. Reviews are essential!

(2) Become a VIP

VIP's are what I call the people on my mailing list. They get latest updates on book releases, blog posts, and (best of all... wait for it) FREE GIVE-AWAYS!

Become a VIP today.

(3) Get Next Book in Antique Assassin Series

The adventures of Dexter and John continue in *Hired Gun (Book 1)*, *Stranger Danger (Book 2)*, *Color Blind (Book 3)*. Dexter and John find themselves protecting LeClaire from crime families, racist groups, family members, serial killers, and themselves. Find these titles where books are sold.

Thanks for your help, and thanks for reading!

Cheers,

Ryan J. Pelton

About the Author

Ryan J. Pelton is a genre-hopping author with over seventeen fiction and nonfiction titles to date. He also hosts a popular writing and publishing podcast (TheProlificWriter.net). Ryan reads, writes, naps, dreams, and nurses a Diet Coke addiction with his wife and four children in Kansas City, Missouri. Email Ryan and say hello: RyanJPelton.com/fiction